The Fine Round Cake

Four Winds Press · Macmillan Publishing Company
866 Third Avenue, New York, NY 10022
First published 1991 in Germany by Verlag J.F. Schreiber GmbH, Esslingen
First American Edition 1991
Printed and bound in Belgium
10 9 8 7 6 5 4 3 2 1

The text of this book is set in 17 point Goudy Old Style.
Typography by Christy Hale

Library of Congress Cataloging-in-Publication Data is available.
ISBN 0-02-733568-2

The Fine Round Cake

ADAPTED BY ARNICA ESTERL
FROM THE JOSEPH JACOBS STORY "JOHNNY-CAKE"
TRANSLATED BY PAULINE HEJL
ILLUSTRATED BY ANDREJ DUGIN AND OLGA DUGINA

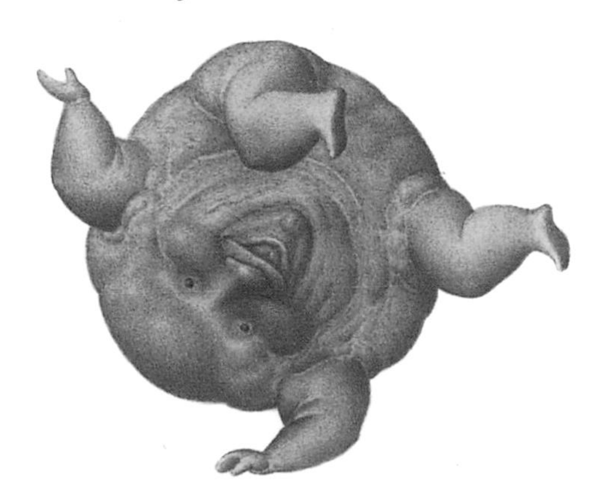

FOUR WINDS PRESS NEW YORK
MAXWELL MACMILLAN INTERNATIONAL PUBLISHING GROUP
NEW YORK OXFORD SINGAPORE SYDNEY

Once upon a time there was an old man and an old woman, and they had a little son. One morning the wife wanted to bake a cake, so she took eggs and butter, milk and flour, and made a fine round cake. Then she put it in the oven to bake.

"Stay here and watch the cake while your father and I work in the garden," she told the boy. So the old man and the old woman went out and began to hoe potatoes, leaving the little boy in front of the oven.

It didn't take long before his stomach started to rumble. Oh, how he'd love to try the cake! He opened the oven door just a tiny bit to peek inside. But in a flash, the fine round cake

jumped out of the oven and went
rolling right out the door!

The little boy ran after it, but the cake was faster. It rolled and rolled away down the road before the little boy could catch it.

He shouted for his father and mother, and hearing the noise, they threw down their hoes and ran to their son. But the cake rolled away from all three of them, and after a while, they had to sit down at the edge of the road to catch their breath.

The cake rolled on and on, and by and by it rolled past two men who were digging a well. "Cake, fine round cake, where are you going?" they asked.

The cake answered, "I've run away from an old man and an old woman, I've run away from a little boy, and I'll run away from you, too!" And away it rolled. The men threw down their shovels and ran after it. But they couldn't catch it, and after a while they had to sit down to rest.

The round cake rolled on and on, and by and by it met two girls who were gathering red berries. "Cake, fine round cake," they cried, "where are you going?"

"I've run away from an old man and an old woman, I've run away from a little boy and two well-diggers, and I'll run away from you, too!" the cake answered, and rolled on. The girls ran after it, but they couldn't catch it. After a while they sat down, ate their berries, and rested.

The round cake rolled on, and by and by it met a bear. "Where are you going, fine round cake?" the bear asked.

"I've run away from an old man and an old woman, I've run away from a little boy, two well-diggers, and two girls with red berries, and I'll run away from you, too!" said the cake.

"You will, will you?" the bear growled. "We'll see about that!" and he trotted after the cake. But it rolled on and on and soon disappeared round the bend of the road, so the bear stretched out to take a rest.

On and on went the cake, and by and by it met a wolf. The wolf asked, "Fine round cake, where are you going?"

"I've run away from an old man and an old woman, I've run away from a little boy, two well-diggers, and two girls with red berries, I've escaped from the bear, and I'll run away from you, too!"

"You will, will you?" snarled the wolf. "We'll see about that!" and he ran after the cake with great leaps. But it rolled away so fast that the wolf had to give up the chase, and he, too, lay down to rest.

The round cake rolled on, until at last it came to a fox that was lying lazily in the shade of a hedge. "Ah, fine round cake, where are you going?" the fox asked, without rising.

"I've run away from an old man and an old woman, I've run away from a little boy, two well-diggers, and two girls with red berries, I've escaped from the bear and the wolf, and I'll certainly run away from you, too!"

"Ah, fine round cake, I can't quite hear what you say. Won't you come a bit closer?" the fox asked.

For the first time the cake stopped rolling. It went a little closer and shouted in a very loud voice, "I've run away from an old man and an old woman, I've run away from a little boy, two well-diggers, and two girls with red berries, I've escaped from the bear and the wolf, and I'll certainly run away from you, too!"

"Ah, fine round cake, I still can't quite hear you. Won't you come a *bit* closer?"

The round cake now came quite close, bent over the fox, and—*snap*! In the twinkling of an eye, the fox grabbed the cake with her sharp teeth and gobbled it up!